DATE DUE			

Would You Wear a Snake?

Distributed to Schools and Libraries
in Canada by
SAUNDERS BOOK COMPANY
Box 308
Collingwood, Ontario, Canada 69Y3Z7 / (800) 461-9120

Library of Congress Cataloging-in-Publication Data
Woodworth, Viki.
Would you wear a snake? / Viki Woodworth.
p. cm.
Summary: Presents in rhyme both humorous and realistic suggestions
for clothing in various situations.
ISBN 0-89565-821-6
[1. Clothing and dress – Fiction. 2. Stories in rhyme.]
I. Title.
PZ8.3.W893Wp 1993   91-34785
[E]–dc20   CIP / AC

WOULD YOU WEAR A SNAKE?

by Viki
Woodworth

THE
CHILD'S
WORLD

Viki
Woodworth

Viki Woodworth graduated from Miami University in Oxford, Ohio. Though trained as an art teacher, she chose to write and illustrate children's books as a way to teach and reach children. She lives in Seattle, Washington with her husband and two young daughters.

**What would you wear
as you splash in water?**

A shell?

A swimsuit?

A tub
or an otter?

(A Swimsuit)

What warms your hands while you tumble in snow?

A pepper?
A porcupine?
Mittens
or bows?

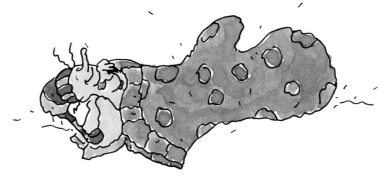

(Mittens)

What keeps you dry when the rain pours down?

An umbrella?
A flute?

**A kettle
or a clown?**

(An Umbrella)

What covers your feet
when you jump in the mud?

A snake?
A banana?

**Boots
or a bud?**

(Boots)

What will you wear when you go out to play?

Take a look outside.

It depends on the day!